MACABRE LADIES PUBLISHING

Drabbles of Dread

A Horror Anthology

This book was professionally typeset on Reedsy.
Find out more at reedsy.com

Contents

Acknowledgement

This one's for COVID.
Ah, just playing. Fuck you COVID.
This one's for all the amazing books out there that saw us
through this bullshit.

1

Broken Bones by Eleanor Merry

A visceral scream tore through her throat, shredding her vocal cords. She could still hear the audible snap, though, followed by the blinding pain of bone breaking through flesh.

Her body shook as she sobbed, sharp stabs up her leg with every motion. After a few moments, she calmed herself slightly, though the pain was just as bad.

It was then she realized it was getting dark and a shiver not from the cold crept up her spine. She could smell her own blood, hot and coppery in the cool night.

Howls in the distance told her she wasn't alone.

2

A Rough Way to Go by Chris Miller

The shards danced about him as he tumbled, eyes bulging, mouth open in a hissing wail of terror, agony, and surprise. His entrails whipped as the ruined window flew higher, his killer's sadistic smile adorning its center.

He pitched, now seeing the street rushing up at him. The hiss evolved into something indecipherable when his guts went taut, catching on the streetlamp, and his body lurched forward, slowing.

At least I won't ruin my car, was his final thought.

His face cratered the side of the car, shearing off his head as his body dangled from the streetlamp, quivering, dripping.

3

Ink by Alanna Robertson-Webb

Celina sighed, glaring at the crumpled, crimson-stained wads of parchment strewn about. How was she supposed to write a love letter when she could not think straight?

She tried again, dipping her pen into the liquid, but her trembling hands failed her.

The world started to go dark.

She lay her head on the table in defeat, ignoring the pain lacing her arms. Celina had wanted this letter to be special, to show Garth just how much she could not afford to lose him, but mayhaps using one's own blood to write a letter in was not a good idea.

4

Assisted Suicide by Natasha Sinclair

"Yes." Seductively biting her rouged lower lip.

"Really! Thank you, I wouldn't want it to be anyone else, honestly."

He lay back, eager, on the black damask sheets as she took in the sight of him. *He had begged enough.*

Crawling up on the bed, a majestic sexual predator. She glided her body against his, breasts caressing his chest before taking position. Latex-clad thighs spread at either side of his face.

Looking down at him, eyebrow arched, "Ready?"

"Ready." His voice cracked with anticipation.

She lowered her sex, letting him lick before covering his mouth and nose; sweet suffocating death.

5

For A Moment by Chris Bannor

For a single moment, there was peace and I forgot the pain and horror of life. I felt as one with the waves that embraced my body and had always - always - pulled at my spirit.

In that split second, I was more at peace than I'd ever been.

Then I remembered where I was. His hands at my throat. Holding me down. Moments of lucidity fleeting and visceral in ways they weren't at any other time in my life. Horror filled me as I gasped, and water filled my lungs. I clawed at the arms above me.

Please….

6

The Door To Elsewhere by Leon Sluyter

The door appeared overnight. It must have. Yesterday when they played in the basement, it did not exist. The twins were sure of that.

"I dare you to knock on it." Katy refused, she felt scared beyond belief.

"Then I'll do it!" Suzy said to terrify her sister some more.

"There's no need to be afraid, children."

A calm, tranquil voice travelled through the door.

"Who are you?" The twins exclaimed simultaneously.

"I am Moloch and I love children, all you have to do is welcome me."

Suzy said; "Welcome."

The door cracked open, and Moloch dragged them to Gehenna.

7

Good Morning By Jacek Wilkos

He crawled to the bathroom like a zombie. He still wasn't used to getting up early. Staring blankly at the mirror for a moment, he splashed his face with cold water.

That didn't work.

He opened his eyes and did a double take, not believing what he saw. In the looking glass, he had completely closed eyelids. He rubbed his eyes and looked again. Now he was looking at his reflection as intensely as it did at him.

"I need to sleep more, I have delusions," he thought.

"I need to sleep more, I react too slow," thought the doppel-ganger.

8

Two Went Into the Woods by David Green

"There's a serial killer in these woods?" Alanna murmured, glancing around at the trees.

Brett laughed, his voice echoing through the darkness.

"Does he wear a hockey mask and carry a machete?"

Alanna shrugged. They hadn't been together long, and a secluded area suited their purpose. Brett pressed her up against the bark of an oak tree, stooping to kiss her throat as he ran his hands over her body.

"Who said the killer is a 'he'?" Alanna asked, plunging the knife into Brett's neck.

She grinned as he sank to his knees, fresh blood gushing to the forest floor.

9

Necro Zombie by Natasha Sinclair

A localised thrill of erratic movement around my hard dick buried deep inside my frozen cold seductress. She was underground long enough for the crawlies to move in. Ecstasy exploded, wild sparks danced across my skin, pouring hot inside her cold as I groaned and arched letting it ripple through like a consuming tide.

Looking back down —her jaws spread wide snapping, eyes dead still. Confusion consumes as she buries her face into my belly, teeth grazing my ribcage while clawing furiously at my back. She rips through me, ferocious and wild. My hot blood bathes her grey skin red.

10

Dull Blades by Chris Bonner

Dull blades
   Blood cakes on like rust
   Cuts and thrusts cuts and thrusts
   Floor boards blush
   Drag them up
   hearts and lungs stomach's guts just poke once
   BLOOD
   Bubbling up bubbling up fucking pumped another cut
   Little pieces in the tub sawing cutting chopping stumps
   Red won't leave I scrub and scrub
   Acid bleach ammonia rub
   FUCK
   hussshhh
   Footsteps crunch leaves are crushed
   Scrub again in case they dust
   Just this once the voices shush
   SILENCE ISN'T ANY FUN
   Violent menace many come cherries flash I hear them run

Rusty knives meet shiny guns
Just this once we've just begun

11

Waiting by M. Ennenbach

An hour and a half. Not including the time, I arrived early. Hell, add in the hours I spent staring at the ceiling instead of sleeping.

Cancer.

How the fuck do you tell someone they may have cancer and then make them fucking wait for the results? Hypocritical Oath. Prick.

I feel like shit. Exhaustion. Stress.

Maybe Cancer.

Now my ass hurts from the uncomfortable couch. I've drunk seven cups of shitty coffee.

I may be dying.

I didn't tell Cyndi. Why? Have her feel the same way I do? Scared to fucking death. Frustrated. Waiting…

"Sir? He's ready now."

12

Flipped Drawer by Jason Myers

"You know I don't believe in ghosts, Tom. I'm not a baby and I'm not fucking gullible." Sarah snipped at her husband. "It's bad enough you got me in this dusty ass cabin. I swear I am never letting you search for an Airbnb, cheap asshole."

"Then explain this to me, Sarah. How would a human put all the silverware upside down in the drawer?" Tom shot back. "Try that one for yourself." He pointed at another drawer.

Sarah walked cautiously to the right drawer. She opened it. An orchestra of utensils fell from the upside-down kitchen drawer's tray.

13

End Of It All by Benjamin Chadwick

"Welp, it finally fucking happened." Jesse turned to Carrie looking for a sign of interest in what he said.

There wasn't any.

"The end of the goddamn world baby. Cities fallen. Governments toppled. The dead going around eating people. And all the beer is warm because the power is off."

Jesse threw the can of booze off the balcony and watched it fall to the concrete below. The ravenous infected swarmed to the spot, eagerly looking up at possible prey.

"Fuck it all!" Jesse threw himself off the balcony landing in the crowd. Carrie didn't care. She was already dead

14

Allergic to Monogamy by N.M. Brown

A cupcake sits lovingly on my bedside table. My wife Sheri had to work tonight. This was her way of showing love since she couldn't be home.

Guilt lines my stomach, burning away at my ability to feel joy like acid. But, today's not the day to dwell on past mistakes.

The first bite confuses me, sweet but savory. Red cake crumb remnants say its red velvet, but the taste is off.

My throat thickens as my vision blurs from swelling. I pick up the note. Red velvet peanut butter cake, for the girl with too much love for monogamy.

15

Little Lucy by Cassandra Angler

Little Lucy walked down the hallway, her blanket trailing her as she held it tight against her cheek. Something hit the floor in her parent's room with a wet thud. As she entered the room, Lucy stopped. Her mother stood at the end of the bed, darkness staining the length of her arms. Her father lay on his back on the bed, his face contorted into a permanent scream.

"Mommy?"

Her mother turned to her with pain in her eyes. "I'm so sorry baby." In one stroke she slit her own throat.

Lucy was still screaming when the cops came.

16

Monster Under The Bed by Wendy Cheairs

The man I met came inside the room. He came to me, chose me. I wanted to run; fear paralyzed me into the corner of my daybed. Pulling the pale-yellow pillow between us, he sat on the edge, taking all the space in the small room. He touched my arm, lightly, my skin turned clammy, whispering he would live here now, under my bed.

Screaming, I ran down that hall to tell my parents about him to be told, once again, there were no monsters under my bed and had to return to my room where he waiting for me.

17

Dirt by M. Ennenbach

As the first shovelful of dirt rained down upon the wooden lid, he began to stir. The sound of thunder crackled above. He could see nothing. His arms pinned to his sides. At first he thought it was rain, sleep paralysis. Then his hands found the satin lining. The darkness became suffocating. He worked his arms into motion and began pounding the cushioned ceiling inches from his face. His screams drowned out by the thunder as the dirt fell. Soon there was nothing but his labored breathing. The world went silent.

Was it a dream?

"No," an evil voice whispered.

18

Mr Popular by Galina Trefil

Only the disabled kids and the nerds developed strange powers like pyrokinesis. But Lucas was a handsome, popular jock, so what the Hell?

He glared at the outcasts sitting off to the side in the high school cafeteria. His envy of their comparative normalcy burned.

But he had to contain his fury or…or…. Shit! He smelled smoke. Not again!

With an agonized cry, he fled the room in search of water, hands scalding.

A watching witch smirked, knowing it was only a matter of time before Lucas' rage caused his clothing to catch fire. The arrogant jerk had this coming.

19

Roaches by Jason Myers

"Mr. Roles, you're CT Scan results are in." Doctor Schook loaded the images on the screen. "This explains the constant migraines and vision blurring." Roles examined the pictures of his head on the computer and was rendered utterly speechless.

"It seems that cockroaches have burrowed through your inner ear and laid eggs inside your temporal lobe. That spot," he pointed with his finger, "is the egg sac. We were unsuccessful in removing the sac. The host has retreated even further. I'm afraid there is nothing to do but wait them out."

Roles was already imagining the gun barrel in his mouth.

20

Moloch's Side Of The Door by Leon Sluyter

Moloch was in a jolly mood. He stoked the fires of his furnace to immeasurable heights, while he prepared to lure the twins into his blazing lair in Gehenna.

A few days ago he heard a noise from his side of the veil that divided earth and hell.

He was excited to hear the twins present on the other side.

So overnight he let the door appear and waited for the knock on the door. When it came at last, he assured them he loved children. He cracked open the door and threw the screaming twins into the fiery furnace.

21

The Sacrifice by K. T. Tate

I'm sobbing, kicking as they tie me to their altar. The cloaked figures leer, expecting a turn after their God. But I've seen their masked leader. Jeff is no God.

Symbols drawn they start chanting. I pray to whatever listens. Candle flames turn blue as blackness, thick and bubbling starts to coalesce. Manifesting, gloriously inhuman, I'm awed by its presence.

Some run, some vomit. They obviously never expected their ritual to work. Terrible and magnificent I welcome it. I'm undone by its touch, irrevocably changed. Blessed and empowered my bonds dissolve.

Smiling, I remove Jeff's heart. A fitting first sacrifice.

22

Initiation by A.B. Archambault

"'This I vow."

The words rang out loud and clear, then faded to a soft echo in the cavernous room. Silence ultimately remained, with her partner Dark. Candles flickered in a series of circles, licking against Dark's edges, casting grotesque shadow children against the walls.

I focused on the Master, not seeing the needle near. A sudden burn replaced by pain, as the stitching commenced. I was warned. Lines of steady black sealing blood slick lips. Seamstress is relentless in her pace; Guard's arms like steel don't let me flinch; Master's eyes like candle flame. No sound, this we vowed.

23

Father Not Father by VikingDaddy

My Father became very distant when we lost my Mother.
She did not go, well. There was very much pain.
We gave her, to flame. Ashes returned to Mother Nature.
After, my father spent his days sharpening his trusted Axe.
He said Mother protected us from *them*, while we worked.
I found him one morning standing at the tree line.
Weeks went by and he continued this process almost daily.
One morning he wasn't there, he didn't return for days.
Upon his arrival, he walked me *to* the tree line.

I awoke some time later, and stepped *from* the trees.

24

The Prisoner Of Infinity by Christopher T. Dabrowski

They didn't like each other. He got an e-mail from him.

Should I open it or not?

The curiosity won. There was no content, only a link...
Intrigued, he clicked on it.

He found himself inside the head as if he were a brain.
Confused, he ordered his hands to click. Link moved him
to deeper layers of consciousness—he saw himself trapped in
the head.

Again he had clicked on the link. It took him even deeper
into the self. The subconscious impulse ordered the signal to
be sent out so that he could click on the link again.

25

Rude Awakening by David Green

Danny's eyes opened.

Lights above glared back. He squinted, trying to make sense of his surroundings. His brain told his arm to move, to shield his vision. It refused.

A sensation tugged at his stomach, like urgent fingers poking at his midriff. Danny tried to lift his head. No response.

His vision coloured. He titled his eyes downwards and let out a silent scream, his jaw remaining clamped.

Two figures rummaged through his intestines, the skin of his stomach peeled back, exposing the organs within.

"He's awake!" one of them cried.

"So what?" the other replied. "He'll soon be dead."

26

Extreme Fitness by Lance Dale

Jim went to the side of the trail, hunched over, and gasped for air. His heart raced. Sweat stung his eyes.

"Come on Jim! Keep up! We've barely started." shouted Steve.

"Why did I sign up for this bullshit personal training? Fuck you Steve."

"Let's go!" Steve persisted.

As Jim started, he heard something and stopped. Someone dropped their phone. He answered it and a loud bang rang out. Steve's head erupted and filled the air with red mist.

"Welcome to Extreme Fitness, Jim," said the voice on the phone. "Your checkpoint is in one mile. You have 10 minutes."

27

Wake Up by Mark Anthony Smith

My sister is talking for me again. I can speak for myself. But I can't get a word in edge ways as they sob and blow their noses.

I've never been to a wake before. They're all dressed in black. My Grandma is trying to chew a ham sandwich. I can see her throat is dry. The coffin on the trestle looks ominous. It looks so solid and final. It mutes conversations. Apart from my sister Kate's; she can't stand silence. I feel uncomfortable sat on the deep sofa. I lunge at the open burial box. Gasping, I see myself.

28

The Itch You Can't Scratch by Nicole Henning

I hear the scratching coming from the walls, it wants to get in. I lock all the windows and triple check the door. The scratching follows me as I pace the floors while biting my nails. I can almost feel every jagged line it puts into the siding.

I sit in the middle of the living room floor and rock, as far away from the terrible sound as I can be. The lights go out, the scratching is louder and coming from inside the room now. I stop rocking and scream in pain, now the scratching is inside of me.

29

Fun Guy Funeral by M Betterelli

Oh your growth will keep me warm and hidden as
I lay here quiet, safe, and unnoticed under this tree.
I can feel your volva lightly pressing down on me,
I accept you all into me like long lost friends.
I was abused, discarded, and unwanted till you found me,
but I will never be alone, because you need me
Your stem will be strong, and straight, and stretch high,
while your cap will spread and bloom lovingly shading me.
We merge together symbiotically lending our strengths to one
another,
now please spore and spread my ashes into this world.

30

Grenfell by C. Marry Hultman

It began when she moved in. Dressed all in crimson and with fiery red hair. Her wiles and the movement of her body seduced the husbands, and some wives. Then she touched the arm of Tauber in 7A. Then Charles in 13F helped her move a couch. Tauber pissed in his mailbox and Charles dumped a litterbox over him. Jones in 2B killed Mrs. Patels tomato plants. When Flynn in 3C shot Needham in 4K, little Hayleigh from 1E gutted the cat of old Schneider in 12B.

The woman smiled as she walked away from the burning apartment complex.

31

Black Swan by Eleanor Merry

Trust me, my love, the voice whispered in her mind.

With even steps, the Maiden dipped her toe into the edge of the fiery pool.

We will worship you for all time.

Her lips turned up as the redness crept up to her ankle, a soothing and warm embrace.

Let the black swan guide you.

Closing her eyes, she stepped forward into the burning lake. The Maiden gasped as the fire began to heat up, no longer sweet caresses. Stabbing agony shot through her as she cried out one last time, the betrayal far sharper than the flames.

Ours forever.

32

Devotion by A.B. Archambault

Gods don't pay attention, or maybe I wasn't devout enough. Each night I cycled through prayers, invoking the big three, regional pantheons, and the little spirits in the woods. But I felt alone. Perhaps I should pick just one.

Tonight, not in whispered words on bended knee, but in raw shouts to the inked-out sky, I pray. Righteousness like red fury pushed out the empty ache. She is the only god I need. Her attention full upon me. I know how to worship now. The sacrifice screamed out to the gods as the athame sank deep. They didn't pay attention.

33

A Drink For the Ages by David Simms

"Can you put down the Absinthe for just one month?"

A head shake. "Humanity doesn't deserve it. Besides, it's imported."

I stared out the window. The world burned. Even the four horsemen had given up the ghost and ridden off into the brimstone-tinged sky.

"Fires, the plague, removal of our souls, locusts, and what the hell was that with the spider squirrels?"

An earth-rumbling chuckle sounded. He embraced me. "That was an accident but it made parks relevant again for a month."

I reached for the ancient bottle. A tentacle swatted me away.

"We're not done yet," Cthulhu grinned.

34

Mommy's Little Monster by K. T. Tate

They love my baby daughter. Always playing with her. Offering to look after her. I'm always tired. They tell me that's normal, that I should rest. Get my strength back.

But they don't feed her. They don't wake up in a cold sweat full of dread. She never cries. But I feel her eyes, dark and hungry. I can't resist her. Can't defend myself. I've tried, only for one of them to remove the pillow from my hands and lead me back to bed.

Little by little she devours me. Soon, I will be gone and she will be theirs.

35

The Red by Nicole Henning

The walls are red, it drips down and soaks the carpet making my feet cold. It squishes between my toes; a squelching sound makes my skin break out in goosebumps. I can hear my heart thudding; my breathing comes in labored pants.

The voices are asleep now, finally stated when the red began to flow. First it came out in a trickle, running down my arms and coating my hands. Then it started to spurt, almost blinding me with its warm spray.

Calmness washes over me as I look at my work, he's still now…It's just me and the red.

36

The Chair by Mary Kiefel

My feet are heavy as I am led toward the small room. Heavier still as each step takes me closer. Closer to where I do not want to go.

I knew this day would come. It was inevitable. And I have no one to blame but myself.

I would give anything to go back in time. To undo what I have done. To start over. If only I hadn't been so careless. The time has come to pay the price.

I see the chair. I have no choice. I sit. I am told

"The dentist will be with you shortly."

37

The First Time, Twice by J.L Boekestein

"This… This is my first time. A woman, I mean," Leonarda said. Dolores' long finger forced Leonarda to look up. The dark-haired woman smiled.

"There is a first for everything." She kissed Leonarda.

Time froze.

I'm kissing a woman! I….

To drown isn't a bad thing.

It was Heaven.

Finally, Dolores tore away.

They both breathed.

"You liked your first kiss?" Dolores asked, smiling wickedly.

"Y… Yes."

Dolores looked the young vampire in the eye. "Drink me. Please." She turned around, offering her throat.

Under her spell, Leonarda bowed forward. To drink from a woman. For the very first time.

38

Perfect by Angela Glover

Lisa rummaged through the medicine cabinet and swallowed two of her mom's Percocet before pulling the thread to tighten the sutures. She swabbed the droplets of blood before tenderly applying the bandages to her face and body.

Standing in the crimson splattered bathroom, Lisa looked in the mirror and was eager to see the new version of herself knowing it will blow the minds of those that shamed her.

"Everything alright in there?"

"Yes, mom!"

Lisa stared in the mirror and thought, *I will be perfect.*

39

Rise of the Cockroach by P.J Blakey-Novis

The apocalypse wasn't like it is in the movies. One day everything seemed normal; the next day I was the last human alive. Everybody else had vanished completely. I spent weeks wandering the streets, searching for survivors but there were none. The skies were empty of birds, no dogs barked – the silence was far from golden. I thought there were no creatures left and how I wish that'd been true.

I'd heard cockroaches could survive anything, but I never knew they would eat anything as well. A swarm of thousands covered every part of me, devouring the last of humanity.

40

Within by Chisto Healy

Bradley heard them. He could always hear them. They were in the walls. They scratched from the other side, thumped against the drywall as they moved. They came to the heating and cooling vents sometimes. He could see their eyes glowering at him from the darkness beyond.

He didn't know what they were, only that hey were there before he was. The house belonged to them. He learned how to live with them, to coexist. They would stay in the walls, allow him to live, to carry on as normal, providing he brought them others to feed upon. He did.

41

Wireless by P.J Blakey-Novis

Almost asleep at midnight, the printer's whirring startled me to consciousness. Living alone, my only thought was that someone had accidentally connected to the wireless printer. I heard a sheet thrown out before the machine fell silent.

I'll look tomorrow.

My alarm shattered a fitful sleep and I clumsily stepped out of bed, moving towards the curtains. My foot touched something, and I almost slipped. Lifting my foot, I peeled away the sheet and stared at it. One red word dominated the paper—DIE!

Puzzled, I tossed it towards the wastepaper basket, unaware that day would be my last.

42

The Temptation by Christopher T. Dabrowski

In the locker room of the fitness club, Karolina noticed an open locker.

She wasn't a thief.

It is said that opportunity makes a thief. Wrong! It's character and…the path of life.

She did not intend to steal, but…. she wanted to feel the adrenaline rush.

She wanted to taste the forbidden fruit.

Adrenaline—the best antidote to boredom.

She desired to invade somebody;s privacy, look at the contents feel the taste of forbidden and…put everything back.

She took a risk.

Something munched. It pulled. Terrible pain. A blood-spurting horrible stump!

The pocket showed its teeth with satisfaction.

43

Waiting by John Buja

I've been under here for a very long time and there's not much left of me. My skin's all gone, but my bones are still here.

That uncle, whose name I don't know, comes back to visit. He kneels on my grave and pulls out his thing and plays with it. Like he used to play with mine. He hurt me a lot because I didn't like it. I promised I'd get him back. He laughed while he strangled me, said, "What can you do?"

I can use my hands to dig.

My teeth are still strong.

I can bite.

44

Karma's a Bitch by Marina Schnierer

Loud cracks of lightning and booming thunder fill the night sky. Feeling my way along the dark corridor, I go in search of some candles.

As I reach the kitchen I am startled by a shadow moving across the room, momentarily revealed by a flash of lightning. About to turn and run another bolt of lightning reveals the intruder before me. A disfigured face so horrific it sickens me.

"Remember me?" The figure asks as she pours liquid over all over me.

Sudden realization that karma had finally caught up to me as I hear the flick of a match.

45

Lightning by M. Ennenbach

the world is silent but i know they are still there
the rumble of thunder above the heavy clouds
a flash of lightning illuminates the still land
as i blink away the afterimages of purple trying to commit the
locations of
their still forms to memory
all is pure fear
one wrong step then they pounce
no one knows where they come from
what they are
just that they hunger
thunder lightning map
i hold my breath shaking as i take one step another
a rock skitters
i hear them race towards me
lightning flashes
all i see is death

46

There are Monsters Under the bed, Jimmy by John Buja

I've been under this bed for hours waiting for my angel. His undies amused me for a while, but now I want him.

There's a noise! He's home, but not alone.

Damn. More waiting.

My angel comes into his room. My knife is ready for our dance of love and death.

His parents are here! Why?

He jumps on the bed and something drops to the floor beside me. A cleaver.

A tiny hand retrieves it.

"Careful, son."

"Let him be, father. It's his first."

His face appears. He smiles.

Those pointed teeth aren't an angel's.

"Hello, mister. Wanna play?"

47

Dreamscape by Chisto Healy

Every time I went to sleep, I would awake to find another piece of my dream in reality. Little by little I was bringing them back with me. With each passing day, my reality was becoming more like the surreal landscape of my daily nightmares.

I would sleep and dream of people being murdered. I would dream of their bloodon my hands. I would hear the sounds of the screams so vividly that they would echo when I awoke.

Each morning, I would rise to find the victim from my dream right there in my bedroom, staring at me.

48

A Weekend Away by David Green

"You're sure no-one will catch us?" The female asked, laying on the bed.

"Who's gonna find us out here?" The male replied, removing his clothing and moving between the female's legs. "Nobody out here for miles. No cell signal, no parents, no worries. It's perfect."

He kissed her, and she ran her hands across his chest and down his stomach.

"Just me and you," she murmured, her voice thick with excitement.

Not true, The Dark Watcher thought, peering through the crack in the closet. It'd waited years for prey to return to its lair. How it hungered for fresh blood.

49

Zombie Burgers by Joshua E. Borgmann

The zombie burger tragedy was largely avoidable.

While the undead turned out to be mostly docile creatures that could easily be herded, there were still millions of them filling the country side, feeding on livestock. An angry farmer is credited with being the first to cannibalize the zombies. Somehow, overzealous corporate researchers labeled cooked zombie meat safe and delicious. The inherent hygienic issues with eating dead flesh were seemingly forgotten as zombie burgers quickly became a massive hit at burger joints everywhere.

Unfortunately, the research failed to reveal that zombie meat was highly addictive and led inevitably to violent insanity.

50

Mary by Angela Glover

The whistling and rattling grew louder as the wind fiercely shook the wooden shack. Mary let out a sigh knowing it was time to move again. She covered her face with a dirty bandanna and large goggles before putting on her heavy backpack.

Windstorms are the only time survivors can search for safety since they diminish the Feeders ability to see and hear. The windy conditions blew debris and sand, Mary withdrew her gun and shoved open the door. Dreading the hike, she reminded herself of the mission and need to protect her growing belly to save civilization.

51

Beloved Beheaded by Mark Young

Crows pecked at mounted heads as guards marched George Widlow towards the chopping block, his hands tied behind his back. He'd stolen a loaf of bread. His family were famished.

They'd already lost little Milly to starvation and couldn't take losing another.

But the sovereignty wouldn't allow criminals to go unpunished. George was to be made an example of.

Led onto the rostrum, he was forced to kneel and place his head on the rest. No last words.

The blade came down. His head rolled, stopping at his wife's feet. Smiling, he said 'goodbye.' And she screamed like never before.

52

The Tree by Mark Anthony Smith

Polly should have met him at the tree. She feels awful for blaming him again. She shouldn't lash out at Kevin. But he's the only one that listens. She cannot accept the blame herself.

She can only feel sadness for her harsh words. She still thinks he deserves it. She could just have been kinder. She phones Kevin but he doesn't answer. He must be sulking under the shade of the big Oak Tree. She throws her arms up and laces her shoes up. She sets out to ask him to apologize. Then she sees him dangling by his neck.

53

Birth by Chris Miller

She curled forward, face red and teeth bared, screaming again. Her hand crushed mine, but I heard the doctor's words and knew it was over.

"I've got him!"

"Him?" she asked as her grip loosened on my hand.

Both our smiles diminished as He stepped from the shadows, holding the knife, his eyes dark. The doctor trembled as he turned, offering up the crying child.

I turned and cupped her face. We wept. There was no other way.

The doctor slipped away as the cries of our baby—never really ours at all—were cut short by the cold blade.

54

Gemma's Teddy by Natasha Sinclair

The breeze wafted through the thick deep orange curtains. Bathing the drab third floor flat. Manky midden air from the rising summer heat mingled with the rising damp of the crumbling tenement walls. A fresh lick of paint only tricked the eyes. Festering rot just beneath that thin surface.

Gemma sat in the corner of the living room, face blotchy red in desperate tears. Huddled into her baby, wrapped in his pale blue teddy blanket. Dead. Still. Rocking back and forth quietly sobbing; "I just needed you to stop screaming, just for a minute."

"You can wake up now, Teddy...."

55

Grave by Justin Scott

I crouch down against the cold mausoleum stone door, hands under armpits against the cold.

I shouldn't have interfered, spying in the night, just left the youngsters to their cheap graveyard thrills.

Breath catches.

Straining towards faint sound.

Not voices.

Singing.

From behind me.

Louder now, and claws scrabbling scraping on stone.

Frozen in place as words clarify, faint but distinct.

Terrible words, promises that seep into my veins like poisoned blood.

I feel the door move behind me.

I run, but they take me down in the dark, claws in my legs and then the pain and screams eternal.

56

No by Leon Sluyter

"It's hard to say no for some people, especially this weeping whore in front of me. But I mustn't digress, let me finish this nasty task up here."

Ramon thought this bitterly, but she knew what he thought of her. He'd made it very clear to her that her cheating days were over.

"So do you feel like cheating on me now?"

But the woman ignored him.

"What's the problem, cat got your tongue? Silence means yes, no?"

She still ignored him, like he predicted.

"It's hard to say no for some people, especially when your mouth is sewn shut..."

57

One Flesh by Mark Anthony Smith

I cut myself open and tear out some entrails. I throw the mess into the shadow. It rasps and wheezes, grasping for more. I should have given my wife due diligence whilst I could.

Now, I hack my leg off as the room swims and I clench my teeth. The bloodied stump is stinging. I fall back in pains. It wants more. I scream disbelief. It echoes its last. I sit up and rummage through my chest. I tear free what looks like my heart. I toss the beating glob.

Then she lurches awkwardly and cackles. Our mismatch engulfs me.

58

Mirror Mirror by Nicole Henning

I've covered all the mirrors and blackened all reflective surfaces. There's nothing they could use to get me in this house. The phones screen is scratched and cracked functional only for ordering delivery. Sitting in a reflection less world and know they are waiting behind the darkness.

The mirror in the hall has been calling to me, one corner of the tape has rolled up leaving a 1-inch square of bright reflection. I tried to ignore it but I looked, then screaming I'm sucked back into the mirror, to wait for someone to remove the tape and let me out.

59

Playdate by N.M. Brown

We started taking our six-year-old to therapy a month ago because of his imaginary friend. He'd have violent outbursts; his tantrums carried the weight of a grown man's. He would do the most evil things. The slaughtered animals forced professional intervention. We'd never see it happen, just clean the devastation afterwards. His explanation was always the same, "Masha did it!!"

I hugged my son Brendan as we got home from today's session. "Did that make you feel any better honey?" I ask tentatively.

His face lights up when he looks out the window as the doorbell rings, "Mom! Masha's here!"

60

Lean Cuts by Chris Bannor

Campus shut down at night, but there were always stragglers. Late night students dashing out at the last moment to finish a project, secret rendezvous between young co-eds with no money and too many hormones to wait until their roommates were gone.

He watched them scurry away like mice, never seeing the hawk in their midst. He eyed them all, looking for the strongest and leanest. He liked the way they fought before they felt the slide of metal and the pull of lethargy.

He liked the way their flesh cut and how it cooked. He liked his meat lean.

61

The Debutante by Charlotte O' Farrell

Your generation find debutante balls archaic, right?

Well, they've always been part of this town's heritage. My own introduction to polite society was nearly 60 years ago but I remember it so clearly.

Meredith was the undisputed belle. When she walked in, all eyes turned to her. All chatter stopped. She moved elegantly into the middle of the dance floor. The rest of us girls avoided her eyes.

This was her 80th debutante ball.

She picked out the shy blonde girl at the back: Emma.

"That one," she hissed, licking her fangs at the thought of another dose of youth.

62

The Beast by Tara Losacano

I'm so tired. I've been running for hours, only stopping long enough to catch my breath. Then I hear the thumping footsteps close by and have to run again.

The beast first found me at my campsite while waiting for my husband to return from collecting firewood. The sun had just set. The beast stepped out of the trees, his horns dripping in blood.

I have to stop again, I have no energy left. I hear him coming. He's here now, glaring at me with his angry, red eyes. I close my own eyes tight and wait for his wrath.

63

Get Away by Galina Trefil

A ghost is in your house? You move. It's that simple.

But this was a crappy old trailer in an even crappier trailer park. Move out? If only!

The family had known about the murder before they'd moved in. But this broken-windowed, stained-floored crime scene was all they could afford.

"Someday, I'm going to get away from here," their daughter vowed.

In response, her homework levitated into the air, only to be shredded. An invisible hand slapped her hard in the face.

"I'm going to get away," she stubbornly repeated.

Both she and the ghost knew that she was wrong.

64

Blood Rush by Jason Myers

The motorcycle helmet Sam wore as she rode her dirt bike felt a little snug on her ears but she was determined to ride before the storm. Equipped with bluetooth speakers in the helmet, she cranked Killswitch Engage and kickstarted the bike. It roared to life and she took off through the field in her backyard. Between the storm coming and the tunes, her headache was rising.

Unable to quickly strip the helmet, she adjusted the speakers. Turning the dial the wrong way, the volume reached maximum and instantly ruptured her eardrums, blood rushed from them—rendering Sam forever deaf.

65

Grave Issues In The Graveyard by Andrew Kurtz

The young woman stood in the cemetery at midnight. She heard the soft sounds of footsteps and turned around.

It was a man in torn clothes, with maggots covering his body. His skin was decayed and sliding off his face, revealing rotting bone underneath. One eye was hanging by its membrane.

As the creature approached, she gouged out a chunk of flesh from his neck with her teeth and started chewing on it.

"I quit!" the zombie actor screamed, blood gushing from his neck.

"That is the last time I hire a ghoul as an actress," muttered the film director.

66

Moloch's Deceit by Leon Sluyter

Sharon smiled as she heard the brats scream when Moloch dragged them off.

Now she could live the life she always wanted, because of the gold Moloch promised for her lovely twins.

"First, I go to the water park to relax for a little while." Sharon thought.

As she glided down the waterslide, a malfunction paralyzed Sharon from the neck down. Sharon sued the water park and settled for a sum of twenty million dollars.

Depressed, she sat at home and cursed Moloch.

"You got what you wanted, you're rich enjoy it." Moloch mocked the handicapped woman and disappeared laughing.

67

Date Night by Marina Schnierer

Blind dates never usually worked out well for Danny but this woman was gorgeous with a killer personality.

She invited him back to her place for a night cap and upon entering her apartment, he was surprised by dozens of mannequins in various positions around the room.

Distracted by her moving in for a passionate kiss, Danny relaxed. Suddenly he felt a sharp sting. He opened his eyes and was startled by her sinister grin and a needle in her hand. As he became woozy the last thing Danny saw before passing out were the mannequins moving in towards him.

Guilty Conscious by Nicole Henning

I see you everywhere I look. At the bank and the park. In the reflections on strangers' sunglasses. Your face frozen in fear, staring back at me; mocking me at every opportunity.

I tell myself that it is just my mind playing tricks on me. A PTSD symptom from all the abuse and endless berating's. Your words echo in my mind throwing themselves against the walls of my brain. Once home I get out the saw and move the blanket off your grey face. Your lifeless eyes look up at me, I'm going to take that look off your face.

69

The Conversation by Chisto Healy

Peter looked at Mark. "You didn't do anything wrong," he said.

Mark frowned. He had tears in his eyes. "She's dead. It's my fault."

"No. It's not your fault. She made you do it. She found the others. Mark, you had no choice."

Mark considered these words for a moment but knew despite it all they were merely platitudes. It *was* his fault and he *did* kill her,

"I had a choice, Peter. Every time, I choose to kill."

"Mark, I need you to listen to me…"

"I always listen to you, Peter. That's the problem. You aren't even real."

70

Parasite by K. T. Tate

Your chest tightens. Gasping, coughing as confusion spreads. Panic cascades.

Desperately you gulp but air evades you. You try to drink but to no avail. Your mind is racing. You know you're going to die. Tears fill your eyes.

Nestled invisible in your chest I revel in the ecstasy of filling your lungs and giving you nothing. As you writhe, choking, wheezing, I feed. Your dread a cornucopia of suffering, such a delicacy.

Then, suddenly, I'm gone. Satisfied, I flop from your airways, engorged. You inhale deeply. Such relief, such tears of joy. You'll be ok. Until I'm hungry again.

71

Through The Broken Windshield by C. Marry Hultman

The headlights flashed on and off. The horn, stuck, blared its eerie foghorn note into the darkness of night. Scorch marks marred the trunk of the tree he'd hit. Lucas tried to move from the seat but was trapped.

He had swerved at something on the road. What though?

A child.

There was a child on the road.

Shapes emerged from the dark. Small figures climbing over his vehicle. They slowly became visible in headlights. Children with pale skin and black eyes, crawling towards him, touching the windshield. He struggled and screamed into the night as the car door opened.

72

The Ghost Of Yonder Redtree by Patrick C. Harrison III

An old Apache named Yonder Redtree lived in the woods. Off the trails and through the briar, his little shack stood. Bountiful whispered fables affixed to Yonder Redtree.

Townsfolk and inventive young boys, pinned him a loon, a witch, a cannibal by decree. When droughts downed crops and diseases filled graves, it was Yonder Redtree who retained blame.

Thus, with torches, weapons, and rope, the townsfolk came. They cursed him and beat him and hung him from a birch. But the sin of the townsfolk birthed a curse: through their roads, homes, and crops, the ghost of Yonder Redtree lurks.

Previous Residents by Chris Bannor

The house smelled new, like fresh paint and recently landscaped lawns. The neighborhood was quiet with high fences between homes for privacy but where they brought casseroles over for the new family. She sat on the back porch, sipping tea and watching fireflies dance across the night when she heard the first noise. No one explained why the house had sat empty for so long, nor the long history of quick turnovers. The price had been too good for her to question it. She should have.

As the dead began to rise, she wished she'd known about the necromancer's graveyard.

A Recipe For Revenge by David Green

Ruth arrived at the Coulson's front door, her sanitary mask hiding a grin.

For years, those in the gated community treated Ruth and her family with contempt.

She'd dealt with rumors, disdain and outright hostility. Their background not reaching the residents exacting standards.

Lock-down presented an ideal chance. Ruth volunteered to prepare meals for the elderly in the community, adding a special ingredient to every order—Ricin. An idea she stole from a TV show. The undetectable poison caused flu-like symptoms then death.

She'd planned it to perfection.

Ruth left the package and strode away, knowing she'd gotten away with murder.

75

The Boogey Man by Tina Merry

My heart would pound walking home in the dark after the winter Brownie meetings. Terrified of what lurked in the woods, Oma's tales helped feed my active young imagination. If I went too close to the woods, something evil would surely get me, so I walked in the middle of the road for protection.

Year later, I wait for the police and more interviews. They found my daughter's decomposing body yesterday. No one can explain the strange marks on her body, but I know it was my fault; I didn't warn her to walk in the middle of the road.

76

Pecking Order by Mark Young

Seeds scattered across the floor towards the open door of Miranda's balcony as she fell.

Unable to move she cried out, but no-one came.

Birds inched into the apartment, pecking at the food. Miranda smiled. Her friends had come to keep her company. Soon they amassed in great numbers and the food was gone. Still they came. And they were hungry.

Peck. Miranda yelped. Peck peck. Claws scratched her face bloody. The birds flocked, covering her body, tearing through her nightie and nipping at her flesh. She screamed. The last thing she saw were two crows coming for her eyes.

77

Nowhere to Hide by Nerisha Kermraj

"I'm coming for you, Melody…"

The whisper sent chills down her spine.

She dropped the phone then, reeling from hyperventilation.

She called Jacob. No answer.

Please let him be alright.

They would have to leave tonight.

She grabbed whatever she could, and headed out to fetch him. But a few meters away from home, her tires screeched to a halt. A battered and bruised man lay across the road, blocking the path.

Her blood ran cold as she recognized the familiar face of her husband, before a gunshot pierced the silence, followed by her deafening screams.

He was already here.

78

Hungry by Galina Trefil

A basement. No windows. One door.

And a huge anaconda in front of that door.

Jeff. That stalking son-of-a-bitch! He'd promised Iris that, if she'd just go out with him once, he'd leave her alone if she still wasn't interested. A roofie later, she woke up here.

"Let me out!" Iris screamed, to no avail.

After several sleepless days, she finally worked up the nerve to approach the door—to escape or die trying!

To her surprise, the well-fed serpent didn't move, ignoring her. But the door was locked.

She stared at the anaconda. How long before it became hungry?

79

R.I.P Van Wikle's Dog by Joshua Borgmann

The dog futilely licked Rip's sleeping face.

"What about the animal," one of the fae asked.

"Throw him a unicorn bone," answered another.

The bone was quite delicious and invigorating.

When the dog returned home, he tried to lead Rip Jr. to his father, but the boy ignored him. They always ignored him. Few even noticed that he remained young while men grew old and colonies became a new nation.

For years, he howled for his master, yet upon finally returning, Rip didn't recognize his loyal dog.

Heartbroken, the dog left to find the fae. He dwells with them forevermore.

80

What Awaits by Tara Losacano

He constantly asked the nurses if he would go to heaven when he died, knowing his long life was almost through. The nurses always reassured him that of course he'd go to heaven. He was a good man, after all. But he knew the truth. He was not a good man.

As he took his last breath and closed his eyes, he felt the burning heat of Hell getting closer. He heard the agonizing screams of the damned. He heard the laughter of his victims, ready for vengeance. Then the pain began and his screams joined the others.

Take An Inch by Chris Hewitt

Trevor was one of those guys you'd give him an inch and he'd take a mile. Okay, maybe not a mile, but more than his fair share. He was the last guy you'd want to be stuck with in a tough situation.

Don't get me wrong. I knew it was coming for weeks and I was willing to do my part, give my part even. Take an inch, I told him. And what does he do? He saws off half my leg.

That's Trevor for you. We were starving to death, I get it, but that's just being bloody greedy.

82

Change at Doncaster by Mark Anthony Smith

Kim doesn't know where he is. The early sun is an assault on his drunken senses. He should have been in London last night, but he was told to change at Doncaster. He is trying to recollect his rickety train of thought.

His hands are bloodied and his shirt is torn. He can hear the commotion out on the platform. There's armed Police. Kim slides across the urine splashed tiles. He looks through the chink in the door. He squints at the bright sun. The station looks like an abattoir. Kim fights back tears. He knows his days are numbered.

83

Hybrid by Scott McGregor

A werewolf, vampire, and zombie walk into a bar.

"How may I help you boys?" asks the bartender.

"I want to eat your flesh," says the werewolf.

"I wish to drink your blood," says the vampire.

"BRAAAAAAAIIIIINNNNNNNNNSSSSS," says the zombie.

The bartender gets bitten from all three.

The following night, the monsters return to the bar, and the bartender is there waiting for them. He looks far different from yesterday. As the bartender glares at the monsters, he finds his flesh, blood, and brains to devour.

That was the last time a werewolf, vampire, and zombie walked into a bar.

84

Nocturnal Pursuit by Chris Bannor

She crouched low, hiding in the alcove of a doorway and behind a fallen trash can. She tried to still her breathing, to make as little noise as possible.

Blood ran from a gash on her leg and her pantyhose stuck painfully where they weren't shredded. Her skirt was more red than beige and she tried not to wonder how much more blood she could lose before she passed out.

She rested her aching rest against the door to stop the spinning. but too late she realized something was wrong. Laughter filled the night air, and darkness took her life.

85

Bedtime by Janine Pipe

There is nothing in the world more frightening than being a parent. Suddenly, a whole entire person depends on you completely to keep them alive.

You dote on them.

When they cry, you ache.

When you can't fix their battles, you feel weak. And when they are frightened, you would move heaven and earth to soothe them.

Unless, you can't.

Because when you arrive to say goodnight, they look scared.

"Check under the bed." they beg. "The boogie man is there."

Rolling your eyes, you acquiesce.

And down there is your child, who whispers, "There's a monster on the bed!"

86

It's Shower Time by M Betterelli

I've always known my mind to play tricks on me,
but as I get older it becomes harder to tell.
What is real, and what is fake in my reality,
but does what I see know what I know now?
Laughing and miming washing yourself, the soap slips from
your hands,
but should I see that, and pick it up?
Your balloon animals are distracting, as water runs down
them,
and you make a sailboat miming it's at sea.
Why do you stand there and watch me bathe,
and I remember your just the creepy clown in the shower.

87

Black-Eyed Boy by P.J Blakey-Novis

I'd found it when I was eight and took it everywhere, the spherical and obsidian lump. I'd pocket it before heading out; I'd even call it my friend. But that was weird—it was just a small, impossibly black ball. It was always with me until it wasn't with me. I'd reached adulthood, discovered alcohol.

Drunkenly, I thought I'd lost the ball. I searched everywhere unsuccessfully. I began to cry. Glancing in the mirror I saw only one blue, puffy eye looking back. The other was impossibly black. My comforter was no longer with me, it was within me.

88

Blind Date by Nicole Henning

It seemed like a good idea at the time, the kind of idea that's exciting and new. Swipe right, weeks of engaging conversations. Then the big step to meet in a public place; to meet face to face. Drinks lead to bringing him back to my place.

Roaming hands and rushing fingers get to work as soon as the door shuts, very disappointing. Fumbling in the darkness and collapsing on the floor. The plastic crinkles under his body, before he can question why my hand breaks through and grabs his heart. He dies in the dark without a fight. Typical.

89

The Rolling Head by Joshua E. Borgmann

Marshall Stevens ignored the Arapaho woman's warnings about the woods. He wasn't scared by missing men or bones found covered with human bite marks. He knew the killer, a wife murderer who'd forced his own children to eat their mother's roasted flesh. He planned to see him dead. As he slept, the head rolled into his camp, slowly creeping toward him. Stevens awoke to find himself staring through tangled hair into the glowing eyes of the murdered woman. Her teeth found his throat, and he was devoured like her murdering husband.

Inside she screamed, forever stuck between repulsion and pleasure.

90

The Night Drama by Christopher T. Dabrowski

They felt weaker by night. Although they felt hungry, they were less willing to hunt.

They were getting slower, every move cost them more effort. The anxiety in the community grew. But no one had the strength to deal with it. In the end, most potential victims escaped.

Sooner or later they stopped being afraid. And they will rebel.

Something has to be done before it's too late.

A human doctor was called in—no vampire knew the profession.

They guaranteed him immunity and a lot of money. He agreed.

I don't want you to worry, but you have anemia.

91

Alive by N.M. Brown

My eyes water as I muster the task of opening them. I find myself disoriented, and hot…so very hot.

Slowly but surely, the table I'm laying on begins to move. Air is nonexistent. The ties relating messages from my brain to my body have been severed.

The last thing I remember is preparing the fish from that new market. Black ichor consumed my mouth as I cut into its soft belly.

I find myself becoming colder as the individualized hairs on my body begin to burn away.

My lungs can't gather enough air to shout that I'm still alive.

92

The Bet by Benjamin Chadwick

Losing a bet can really suck. Winning is the shit. But losing? Screw that.

I'd never lost, though. I'm talented that way. So, did it come as a shock the day I finally lost a bet? Fuck yeah. My mind literally flipped. Like, right out of my skull. My death was the cost of losing the bet.

Pretty steep price wouldn't you agree? But, it is what it is. And what was the bet you ask? That I could withstand a blow to the head from a machete. Hey, I saw it on TV. Thought I would live. Who knew?

93

Clinical Depression by Natasha Sinclair

Spine shattering terror was just a 'side effect,' so the doctors said, but they never experienced the realities of it. The madness induced by this little drug—metrazol.

The dread before; only the mad knew hell was coming.

The world suddenly awash with terror, heart banging against skinny, frail ribs - brutal, painful. Trapped heart battling to escape. Lungs filled with air jagged-agony like the molecules contained broken glass shards. Darkness creeping in around every corner - no matter where frantic, darting eyes flew.

Devilish hell demons crawling out of everything, eyes burning with desire to penetrate and consume the depressed subject.

94

A Debt To Be Paid by Angela Glover

"Stop! Stop! Stop!"

Krissy sat huddled on the floor next to her bed and slammed her fists into her temples. She screamed as tears ran down her face, but the crying grew louder.

Trembling, she stood up and followed the cries to the nursery. She grabbed the doorknob and slowly pushed the door open. The dark room was pierced by the moonlight shining onto the crib.

"Please, no! You can't have him too!"

The crying turned into shrieking. Krissy approached the empty crib and began to weep again.

Her nightgown grew wet as the blood flowed down her legs.

95

Next Door by Janine Pipe

We have new neighbours.
I spy a kennel; a dog, how exciting!
Funny though, I have yet to see it?
It's a large house for just a couple.
Night-time now. I hear whining.
There IS a dog.
I sneak into their yard, I can't help it.
So dark, but the moon lights the way.
Gorgeous golden doggy! Chained up, oh poor thing.
Just a quick pet—argh! Tried to bite me.
Kick back, hear a snap as it lands awkwardly.
Next day, feeling guilty, knock on the door to apologize.
Door slowly opens.
Teenage boy, golden hair, on crutches—grinning.

Ninety Eight Point Six Part One by Ruthann Jagge

"Welcome to Homesales, have to take your temperature, it's procedure."

Her green eyes were calm above the mask as the plastic touched her skin.

"Good to go, have a nice day!"

He flushed as young men do when beauty is close.

Red soles flashed and heels clicked sharply on concrete as she gathered: duct tape, metal buckets, tubing, and heavy canvas.

Her gloved hand passed a black card to pay.

These were rare, he was impressed but the sharp edge sliced his finger.

No one noticed her pushing the cart covered with a dark tarp out the door.

Dr. Ed by Chris Hewitt

Dr Ed rarely made house calls and never to the boondocks at night. On the long drive out to the plantation his thoughts turned to the phone call. The pleading voice from his past. A call he'd dreaded.

Pulling up to the house, it was just as he remembered, right down to his mother standing on the steps. "He's upstairs."

He found Jonah in bed, his ever-present tubes hanging from his afflicted skeleton.

"Of course," said Ed, taking his brother's hand. "I promised."

Feud forgotten, his oath to his brother would always supersede his Hippocratic oath.

"I'm ready," croaked Jonah.

98

Antichrist by David Green

Thunder boomed, causing buildings to tremble at their foundations. Nations rallied, preparing themselves for the war to end all conflict.

Food spoiled, and crops died in the space of minutes. Scientists read reports, jaws slack with disbelief.

Death rode on the horizon, though we didn't look up to see it approach.

The oceans ran crimson, boiling the fish that swam there until none remained alive. Acid fell from the skies. Women wailed, men gnashed their teeth—madness and fear whispered sweet oblivion in our ears.

All this happened on the morning my son arrived into the world. I should have known.

99

Last Night by Mark Anthony Smith

"For the last time Daniel, there's no monster in the wardrobe." My Dad has promised me so many things and not delivered. He almost trips over the toy car I stole as he closes the wooden doors. Then he kneels down by my bed and smooths my hair as my heart races. I love my Dad. He does his best. He'd kill me if he knew about the little pick up truck I pocketed. He tries to allay fears with a soft voice.

He screams. Blood spurts on my wallpaper as a claw cuts his throat.

It's under the bed.

100

Quality Time by Ruthann Jagge

"Honey, remember all the movies with pizza and all that good sex?"

His wife was still screaming at him but she'd stop soon, he had her full attention for a change.

"Then you met that guy online and you told me that you wanted to be with him forever?"

Well, he's right next to you now.

"Some might call it cheating but me, I think I'll just call it quality time and you'll have lots of that with him now."

He blew a kiss as he smoothed over the last shovelful of dirt and walked away whistling.

101

The Chewing by Amber M. Simpson

It's the sound of them chewing that haunts me the most—like that of crinkling tin foil. They feed on the old, like vultures of death, picking bodies clean of their souls.

This one crouches on Ruth Hine's shoulder as I wheel her toward her room. That one clings to George Carlson's back as he shuffles down the hall.

Dark and eyeless, they have only mouths—chew, chewing away.

Each night after work from the nursing home, I lie wide awake in fear—that with each new wrinkle or gray hair I find, it's them chewing on me I'll hear.

102

Oh Father! by Mark Young

Recalling his hedonistic days, Sam longed for the time he'd go out dancing with Joey and the gang; then onto an afterparty or two for the rest of the weekend.

Now, zombies chased him into a dead-end street. His chances were over. Until he spotted a hole in the wall, clambered through and blocked it with rubble.

There was a cry in the dark. What had he let himself in for?

There it was again. But this was no zombie. He edged towards the source and picked up the baby.

"Shit! Now, whoever said gay men can't make good fathers?"

103

Ninety Eight Point Six Part Two by Ruthann Jagge

She was close to him again, her green eyes above the mask were calm.

He tried to smile but the tape was tight.

She smelled like the flowers at his Nan's funeral when she held his hands and lifted his arms higher.

His blood dripped into the metal buckets, he could see it flowing through plastic tubes in his body.

She kissed his forehead: "You're getting cold, we're almost done."

He could only stare silently at the row of shiny black shoes.

One by one she patiently dipped them into the buckets staining the soles red with his life.

104

The Doll Did It by Charlotte O' Farrell

"The doll killed them!" I shouted, my voice echoing around the courtroom. The jury openly laughed. The judge smirked. Honestly, I knew how it sounded—I couldn't blame them.

It was me on trial after all, not the bloodstained china doll they found at the massacre scene.

As I was led away to the cells, I cried my last desperate plea: "Just keep that thing away from the other police evidence!"

Two days later I got a newspaper delivered to my cell. Turns out the local police learnt the hard way that killer supernatural dolls are more deadly with guns.

Unicorns by A.B. Archambalt

Only virgins can catch a unicorn—fair maidens in moonlight glades with golden bridles.

No moon shone on the alley, and she was alone, broken. It wouldn't be long until she was gone.

"Mother grant me vengeance," she whispered.

Something rustled in the garbage, it didn't matter, she closed her eyes against the unanswered prayer. Then, a head laid in her lap with a glowing horn. It plunged deep into her and came back dripping blood. Not long now.

It took her offering. Her last sight its silken tail as it left to hunt. They didn't have long now.

106

Tucked in by David Simms

The blanket shimmered as I shifted in the bed.

They had left me hours ago to serve my penance.

It wove itself into a tight covering within minutes, black bodies entangling as sextets of legs meshed across my flesh. Mandibles lapped at the sweet substance poured by those who condemned me.

I could wait them out, I spat through clenched lips.

They chittered back, mocking me, seeking out entry points where they sensed a greater meal.

Where they found none, the mass soon created them, chewing and building as they devoured the sins within.

Soon, the blanket shivered deep inside.

107

Sweet Tooth by M Betterelli

Holding her mothers hand, she looked hungrily at the machine. Pink swirling strands of joy, spun about in its container.

The operator lay hunched over, contents of his cranium emptied. A brain candy tornado of confectionary delights displayed before them.

It had been a while since they both had eaten.

The girl reached out for a nibble "Graaagh!" she muttered.

Her Mother was unpleased and snarled back sharply "Mrrh Grrrh!"

She deserved being scolded, she didn't have permission to eat.

The world may belong to the dead, but nothing changes; children should listen, not eat sweets, and love their Mother.

108

Bucket List Disaster by Amber M. Simpson

Waves crashed against the moonlit shore as Devon and Sara rolled naked in the sand, close to checking "sex on the beach" off their bucket list. Neither saw the long black tentacle slithering snake-like towards them, until its cold slimy grip reached Devon's ankle.

"What the—"

With a jerk that nearly took his leg off, he was pulled into the ocean, Sara tumbling off him with a startled cry.

"Devon!"

Moments later, he emerged from the water, his movements jerky and strange. Sara ran to his side with a sigh of relief—and was decapitated by his sharp-toothed maw.

109

Eternal Love by Janine Pipe

I lie on the bed, unable to move. That childhood saviour for all evil, the duvet, can do nothing to help me now.

My husband's breathing is laboured, his chest rattling as it moves up and down.

I want to wake him, to unburden my fears but I can't.

As he lays next to me I weep.

Despite his presence, I have never felt so utterly alone. I am frozen in terror, willing dawn to break and the nightmares to end.

Paralyzed, I hear him groan. Soon, soon he will be gone again. After all, he did die last year.

110

Place Your Bats by Chris Hewitt

"Ladies and gentlemen place your bats," said the croupier.

Joshua stared down at the table nervously. Several vicious looking creatures had already been placed alongside some sizeable bets. Pulling Pippa his childhood pet pipistrelle from his shirt pocket, he laid her gently on their lucky number. Beside her he slid a single chip. Their life's savings.

The croupier spun the wheel. The first clack of marble against wood and the table erupted into a frenzy of wings, teeth and claws. Blood splattered the faces of the baying crowd. When the ball finally dropped only Pippa remained. Panting, bloodied and rich!

111

Invocation by Emma K. Leadley

"Can you fill the woodbasket?" Emily asked.

James rolled his eyes but shuffled obligingly down the garden in his dressing gown and

slippers. Something heavy landed on James' chest and he staggered back. The thing clawed at his eyes and putrid slime filled his mouth, muffling his screams. James passed out. He came to as daylight broke, staggering to the house, hollering for Emily. In the kitchen, furniture and crockery lay broken. Incense hung heavy in the air and James didn't see the chalked pentagram. All he knew was Emily had disappeared.

But, so had their car and her possessions....

112

Toxic by Benjamin Chadwick

Can a mind be vacant? Will its inner turmoil cease to be? Could the chaos be subdued and tamed? These are the reluctant thoughts of the serial killer haunting the streets. The conscience begs for release while enduring the sights of the grizzly murders being committed by its owner. The cries for help, pleading to end the insanity. But no response is given. This maniacal killer is content. They need no incentive to continue. The sheer lust for carnage is enough. The pulse is pounding in icy veins. And blood…. it craves for it. But the mind is fucking toxic.

113

Boxed In by Marina Schnierer

Darkness all around me, heart pounding, confusion, throbbing pain, barely able to move.

Flat on my back and my head hurts so bad. I lift up slightly and knock my head on something hard just a few inches above. Moving my hands out beside me, I feel the same hard surface either side of me, again only a few inches away.

A drilling sound blasts through the hard surface by my feet followed by a moment of silence. Then a scurrying sound. Horror overwhelms me as I feel dozens of small creatures crawling all over me, nibbling my flesh fiercely.

The Co-Worker by Cher Finver

Ray still e-mails me often, calling me a whore, always ending the communication with a different bible quote. I never reply, reporting every e-mail as instructed. Other than firing him years ago, my agency really has done nothing

I take the stage for my latest book signing. This best-seller is based on the affair I denied that got a certain someone fired. There is an extra place card next to a bottle of water set on a table for me. As the words come in to view, I look around for the nearest exit, "Do everything in love," —Corinthians 16:14.

115

I Left Everything in San Francisco by Cher Finver

I make the pilgrimage to *our* spot. I stand where you proposed, and where we would later marry. Happily married, I thought, until you left. *Our* song in *our* city, "I Left My Heart in San Francisco," plays through my earbuds.

Your note passes through my fingers and a breeze swiftly lifts it up as if to deliver it back to you. The note that explains why you left. *Were you thinking of me right before you hit the water, darling? I hope so.* I am thinking of only you as I let go of the railing, propelling myself forward.

Deep Inside by M. Ennenbach

the lone cry of
the raven
perched
upon the balcony
howls respond
from the wolves
in the dark woods
slowly suffocating
the cottage.
she sits on the edge
of her bed
butcher knife clutched
in her shaking hand
a low chuckle seems
to reverberate along
the very timbers
around her.
"sweetest little dumpling, quivering in delectable dread, fear
not my dearest one, worry not your pretty head,"

"allow me one taste, to run my tongue down your soul, savor
the delightful tint of sin, before devouring your spirit whole"
she nodded
unwilling or unable
to fight against
the dread
inside.

117

Dinner Date by Janine Pipe

Cassie couldn't believe it.

When she'd answered the notice in the newspaper, she had thought it must be too good to be true.

Yet, here she was, in the most high-class restaurant in the entire country.

Feeling extremely nervous. Had spent the entire day pampering and grooming herself.

She could only hope now, that the evening would go smoothly.

As Cassie arrived in the VIP room, there was an audible gasp of pleasure.

The guests applauded her, their mouths salivating.

This, was the world's only cannibal dining establishment. Where nothing was off the menu and tonight, Cassie was the special.

118

The Silence by Chris Hewitt

Have you heard the silence? Sure, you have. Everyone does at some point. You'll be on a train or sitting in a bustling restaurant and for a moment it feels like a bubble of silence passes you by. Like the world has held its breath.

My advice, when it happens again, is do the same. Hold your breath, close your eyes and pray. Don't acknowledge it. Don't ask your loved ones if they hear it. Don't make a sound.

When the universe goes quiet, hide in it.

Don't make the mistake I made. Don't lose them. Don't ever let go.

119

The Eternal Walk by Benjamin Chadwick

Dedicated to my wife Kathy

We walk in the mist
Creatures told thru time
If blood is our endeavor
Than your body is sublime
We peel away the pink flesh
And gorge on the raw meat
Satiating our hunger for now
But a temptation we cannot defeat
Gore covered, we make love
Ravenous in our delights
Betwixt the shadows of nightfall
Another victim is in our sights
Hungry with furious passion
Our lust is bidding
Sharp fangs sink into soft flesh
The thrill of another killing

Our descent into madness
The journey of eternal pain
Taken from my lover
My heart, now just a stain

120

Flatline by Thomas Sturgeon Jr.

Amanda was rushed to the hospital, her life flashing before her eyes. The paramedics kept her alive as they hurriedly went into the hospital. She was already turning blue as the doctors discovered something was wrong with Amanda's heart.

Fear overwhelmed whatever she was as her spirit hovered above her body. The monitors emitted a loud and dooming noise as her heart stopped, and all she could do is look on in horror.

Flatline.

She always knew the consequences of eating too much pork, of never exercising enough. She was crying even in death as Hell appeared before her eyes.

121

Still Life in Art by David Simms

Charley asked Justin if he'd pose for her. An odd duck, but adorable in her way.

If he had asked to see her work, fate may have winked, instead of pissing on him. Yet he could only see the veil of her skin.

If Justin paid attention, he'd have noticed Charley had seen the same.

Her studio invited him as she transformed his body into her palette.

Bodies mixed hues as she prepared, her brushes razors to libidos, her strokes scythes to his form.

At the showing, she displayed him across several canvases, his life, now her art.

122

No Reason by Galina Trefil

Alfred loved his mother. And he hated her too.

But Louise didn't know anything about that. And she didn't notice the anxious stranger ominously following her throughout the supermarket. Later, as she put her groceries into her car, he called out, "Mama!"

Louise didn't turn. Why should she? She didn't have any kids.

She suddenly felt several hard impacts on her back. "Die, bitch!" he shrieked.

She hit the cement, not realizing until she saw the blood begin to pool around her that she'd been stabbed.

Why me? Louise thought.

Alfred ran. The next woman he stabbed wouldn't understand either.

123

Eyes Of Children by M Betterelli

Georgie sat atop the hill overlooking the city down below, his hand raised in the air made into a circle.

"Where'd you come from?" He said curiously to the spider, dangling down between the hole he made with his hand.

"It almost looks like your coming down from the sky!" as Georgia marveled at his friend descending onto the city.

"Are you the big bad monster who's gonna destroy everything?" he playfully said to the spider, now touching the skyscrapers.

Explosions could be heard, along with sirens and screams, but from his perspective it's fake, for them it was reality.

124

Free by Angela Glover

The cackle escaped my lips when I heard the cracking of her bones as I twisted her head from her neck. Miss Gemma's naked body thrashed and kicked against mine before it became limp in my arms. My grasp loosened and she fell to the cold dirt floor in a heavy heap of tangled limbs.

My body began to shake as I sobbed in relief. I looked around the small brick room then up the old wooden stairs to the metal door. What do I do next? I have never been up the stairs before.

125

Madame Darkness by C. Marry Hultman

The screams grew louder behind the locked bathroom door. A concerned crowd had gathered outside.The three girls had gone in there all cocky and self-assured. They had knocked on the mirror six times, flushed the toilet, and called her name three times, urging her to come to them. What had come after that no one knew.

Janitor Langdon finally broke the door down; revealing a grizzly scene of blood-soaked walls spilled guts and a horrible stench. The girls' tiny faces twisted in horrible masks of terror.

A single Queen of Spades bobbing in a crimson pool.

126

Fearless by Chris Hewitt

I know dread. It's a familiar friend. My only comfort in the night. All the while I feel that fear in the pit of my stomach some part of me is still here, still fighting.

Every day I do battle. I can't remember how many skirmishes I've lost. Just like I can't place a name to the faces in the photos on my dresser, recall the day of the week or the name of the dog I hug daily.

I dread the day I lose my fear. That's the day I lose my battle. That's the day my Alzheimer's wins.

127

Killer's Lair by Mark Young

Through blurred eyes, red, white and blue lights glowed in Jimmy's vision. The gurney he was strapped to was lifted into the back of the ambulance. The doors slammed. He was plunged into darkness. Blinking his eyes clear, he tried to sit up but was restrained. The vehicle drove away from the scene of the accident.

Eyes adjusting, confusion dissolved into fear.

Racks of clinking jars containing organs and body parts; rusty tools and antique medical equipment hung on hooks. Despite the pain, Jimmy kicked and screamed for his freedom. This was no ambulance.

But a killer's lair—on wheels.

128

Sober by Angela Glover

It has been one year without the blackouts and missing memories. Chris smiled as he received his bronze chip for sobriety, knowing the alcohol induced nights were now nothing more than a stain to conceal the voices that were only trying to help him.

The sense of accomplishment took over Chris as he pulled the knife from her abdomen and felt the warm blood spill onto his hands. He licked his fingers and reveled in delight as the voices sang to him. Chris smiled knowing he never has to fill the void with alcohol to drown out his desires.

The Sphinx of the Potomac by Joshua E. Borgmann

Nikola Tesla double-checked each motor, gear, and circuit inside his crowning achievement. Convinced that his electronic brain was functional, Tesla sealed the automaton's head. He had to admit its appearance was a stunning copy of the dead man. From the doorway, Secret Service Chief William Moran looked on as Tesla tightened a screw behind the automaton's ear.

It came to life with a lurch and looked around the room. Its face showed no emotion.

Moran asked, "President Coolidge, may I speak to you."

"You just did Mr. Moran," it said.

Moran smiled, "Congratulations Mr. Tesla. This will fool everyone."

130

A Growing Girl by N.M. Brown

My wife ran to me sobbing, her bloodied hands shaking. "Henry, I don't know how I'm supposed to get used to this." She wailed. "LizzyBeth is a monster!"

Squelches and slurps echoed from their daughter's bedroom. "What do you suggest we do? Starve her? We tried supermarket meat; it wasn't enough. This is the only way." I gently reminded her.

"Can't we give them to her after nature's already taken its course? Like picking fresh vegetables from a garden?" She begged, eyes pleading.

"Absolutely not." I balked. "Do you know how many toxic chemicals are involved in the embalming process?"

131

Don't Call Me Mama by Nic Brady

I dread the day my child calls me mama.

I knew I was being abducted. I could feel the microchip in the nape of my neck, in the middle of my fire tattoo. I didn't tell anyone, especially not my husband. He wouldn't understand plus he'd cart me off to the nearest nut house.

There, I fell in love with YVslongo.He had the most amazing blue eyes. The depth I've never before seen. We made love several times.

Now he's gone. I'm left with some semblance of a child, a chip in my neck. That, and dread.

Don't call me mama.

132

Eyes On The Road by Jason Myers

He watched his cell phone screen as the woman was riding the man. Her movement increased in speed as the moaning turned into climaxing. A quick glance up to make sure no traffic ahead. Eyes locked back on his Android as she released again. His tunnel vision locked onto her ecstasy.

By the time he looked up again, his Ford was careening into the pond. His head slammed the steering wheel—instantly unconscious.The cab filled up with icy water rapidly. Muffled screams of her orgasm matched his screams of panic lay on top of the surface with no help around.

133

Misguided Vengence by N.M. Brown

It's the one-year anniversary of my wife Elaine's death. She was killed while taking the neighbor's son Travis to school. Whoever rammed her car off the mountainside didn't even stop afterwards. If they had, maybe our loved ones would've lived.

Since then, I've tried to kill every drunk driver that I can. My Crown Vic looks like the unmarked cop cars here. I pulled them over, and that was that.

I'm home celebrating my thirty-eighth kill in Elaine's honor when I find a note hidden under my desk drawer.

Robert,

It always killed me that Travis had your eyes—-- Elaine

134

Mowed by Cassandra Angler

Lenard pulled the pull chord on the mower, receiving only a sputter from the engine. He flipped the mower back, leaving it standing on its wheels as he examined the underneath.

Lenard grunted, everything free and clear of restriction. He smacked the side of the paneling with all his strength. The engine roared to life, the blades whirling at full speed. Wheels loose from their place in the ground.

Lenard screamed as the blades cut into him, chunks of meat flying through the air and landing in the immaculate green grass. An eyeball dropped into a lemonade glass, Jackie screamed.

135

Ruined by Chris Bannor

She pulled the tatters of her coat over the ruined flesh of her shoulder. Her breath was labored, and her hands shook. Black danced the edge of her vision in a promise of full dark if she wasn't careful.

She couldn't stop. She had come this far to avenge her family. She would never stop hunting the beasts that killed her mother and father, that had made her watch as they drained her brother. They had left her alive, toyed with her, and thought her tamed.

But she would never stop killing them, even if she was one of them.

136

The Legend of John Nuckelavee by Jacek Wilkos

Here's what I've heard: John Nuckelavee was tied on his horse to a lone tree in the middle of the desert. They wound the animal to make it die faster and left him for slow death on a rotting corpse, under the scorching sun.

Their bodies never found.

Shortly afterwards, people started telling about a terrifying nocturnal demon: a man's torso attached to a horse's back, skinless, one animal eye socket empty, the other glowing red like a jewel from hell, looking for his torturers to take revenge.

I'll end this. I'll find those bastards and bring them to John.

137

My Hobby by Jason Myers

"I remember when I first began this, we shall say 'hobby' for lack of a better term. I was so nervous that I actually threw up the first couple of times. Once I got my technique down, however, it became almost like a race to beat my best time. See, the key is to grow your nails out. It helps when trying to grip their windpipe. Once your nails dig into the loose skin around the Adam's apple, there's really nothing to it. They don't scream, merely whimper. Then a quick pull backwards. Success. Windpipe removed with your bare hands."

138

The Shadow by Chisto Healy

Stanley was chopping vegetables for dinner. He couldn't believe Martha was coming over to his house. He had been trying to land a date with her for two years, since they had first met at the office.

He had set the atmosphere and had Italian music playing, and candles as the lighting. It was going to be so romantic, he had it all planned out.

As he chopped the vegetables his eyes found the shadow that splayed across the wall in the candlelight. It was matching his movements. Then it wasn't. As he chopped, the shadow stopped, raising the knife.

139

Last Words by Natasha Sinclair

"You love me more than I love you."

Rippling through the air, words of sadistic poison. It was true—Maria always loved harder than was possible to love her. Cuffed to the St Andrew's Cross—dead words stung sharper than the tails that lashed her reddening thighs, teasing her cunt.

Master knew how to take the pain away. Soon those words would vanish; each strike weakening the torment of the heart.

Nothing cleansed the mind more than complete submission, and nothing purified the exchange than fair coin.

After the session, she would go home and take care of the body.

140

Home by A.B. Archambalt

The house stood faded into the overgrown grass and brush, almost invisible from the street. When the new family moved in, the house was hopeful, maybe it would get new paint, maybe a mow.

The man was spiffy in dark blue suits; the woman candy-colored brittle; the boy too quiet. He whispered to the house, about why his sister wasn't there and concerns too big for a body too small.

When the ambulance took the boy away, the house decided. The gas leaked slowly from rusted pipes, and when the spiffy man lit his cigarette, the house was no more.

Tears by David Simms

Elle first saw the tear on a Monday. Just as the sun struck its apex, a clear glint caught her eye. She approached it, believing it a hung spider of knot of fishing line from a phone wire. Her finger extended into it—and disappeared. Amused, she retracted, studied the hole in reality.

Each day, it expanded, as if a child had pulled on a scab of an itchy wound.

Each day, she reached further. Placed items within.

The cat ruined her. Curiosity bit hard.

Friday, she stepped through the tear. She never saw what caused it.

Or tore her.

142

More by Cassandra Angler

The blade cut into his skin effortlessly. She began to shake with anticipation as crimson stained his pale skin. She looked up at him, eyes begging.

"Go ahead, Love."

She lunged toward the laceration and wrapped her lips around it. Blood pooled on her tongue, her stomach ached.

More.

He screamed as she bit down on the wound. She pulled away from him, sinew dangling from the corner of her mouth as she chewed.

Blood spilled from the corners of his mouth as she leaned in and took another bite. Then another. And another. Full and sated, she slept.

143

A Vow Not Forgotten by David Simms

She's such a bitch, Russ fumed.

Why the hell would she insist on smothering him like this? He'd been there when she needed him, married her when no one else likely would have, allowed her to complete her degree in archaeology.

Miles away from home, she still badgered him.

"Indy-Anna Jones? Who the hell needs that?"

His head pounded from her digs.

Let me breathe, goddamnit.

Why couldn't she leave him be?

All throughout his burial, she had uttered not one word, simply smiling down at him.

The final shovelful of dirt ended their vows.

Finally, he had his peace.

144

The Closet by Chisto Healy

Gary always did a monster check when he put his son, Brian, to bed. It was part of their routine, and almost comical.

Today was different though, because Brian was staying at his mother's for the weekend and Gary was still checking the closet. It was just habit.

He could have sworn he saw something go into it. He saw it with his own eyes. It looked exactly like Brian had described to him so many times. Guilt tugged at Gary's chest, as he moved the clothes, searching around for the monster he had seen.

Unfortunately, it found him first.

145

Last Contact by David Simms

The long gray fingers pointed at the group of men before them.

One by one, they dissipated in a scatter of wet ash.

The final human quivered, praying for mercy, as he surveyed the fruits of his kind's destruction.

Black smoke rose in fiery dances, choking out the life below, the beings the other came to save, withering in its wake.

Those who arrived from above erased much of the planet's cancer within hours, white hot light surgically removing the offense.

The man pleaded, just as those under his gun had done before him, to the same avail.

Intelligent life restored.

146

In The Flesh by M Betterelli

I hit the switch and the machine roared to life,
while the black tenebrous liquid swished around from within.
The vibration was met with the burning sensation of flesh,
and the tingling of senses as to the permanent decision.
The boogeyman hungers for sustenance while his prey is
awake,
but if the cattle are branded, then he stays fed.
It metastasized, and covered the clean palate of her body,
now rendering her helpless to nightmares that stood before
her.
Eyes agape, and panic-stricken, her demons began to terrorize,
much like a fly caught in a spiders web, being consumed.

147

A Mother's Dying Love by Marina Schnierer

Tears flow down the woman's face as she stands over the coffin. She holds a bouquet of flowers in her hand and places them onto the wooden surface.

As the coffin is lowered into the ground, her daughter's favourite song begins to play.

Walking away with her head down after the burial, refusing all offers for comfort, she leaves behind the small crowd.

The woman stops a short distance away and smiles. The smile grows into a sinister grin, followed by a muffled cackle. Gloating that the slow poisoning had done its job, she left the crowd to their bereavement.

148

Possession by Nerisha Kemraj

The eyes of the crystal skull glowed a smoky green. Ian knew he should have left it with the rest of the obsidian mirrors and other artifacts, back at the excavation site near the old temple. He heard all too well about the paranormal phenomena that surrounded the skull, and yet he saw himself drawn to it. Green smoke rose from it, swirling around him.

Ian woke with a jolt, his head heavy. The smell of iron filled his nostrils. He looked at the dagger in his bloodied hands as green smoke lifted from the lifeless bodies of his colleagues.

149

The Hallway of No Return by Kimberly Gray

Kristen Westbrook opened her eyes and found herself in the familiar hallway that plagued her dreams for months. Although she knew what came next, she searched for a way out.

The door up ahead seemed to be an exit, but when she opened it, it only led to another hallway with another door at the end.

Panic set in.

Desperate to get out, Kristen started to run. Each door she opened was only to more hallways and more doors. She ran and ran with no end. When she opened her eyes, she learned she died.

This was her hell.

150

Unheard and Unseen by Marina Schnierer

Invisible, that's how I feel. A strange, almost surreal feeling washes over me.

Large groups of people around me but not one person looks my way. Frustration hits me when I ask what's going on and I am ignored. Am I really so insignificant?

Sirens in the background, getting closer. A scurrying of people as a vehicle with flashing lights pulls up.

Uniformed officers exit the vehicle and the crowd clears the area. What I see next turns my world upside. A body laying on the ground, bleeding, lifeless, and the face, as the body is turned over, is mine!

151

You Were Probably Dreaming by K.T. Tate

There's something under the covers. My feet retract, body backing up until I am against the headboard. I scrabble out of my duvet, desperately flailing for the light switch.

Heartbeat is all I hear as I scan the bed.

Bravery returning, I pull back the duvet.

Nothing.

Unseen limbs grab my feet, pulling me flat. I go to scream but cold fetidness fills my mouth. Blood blossoms up and down my body, staining invisible mouths. I try to kick and fight, but one by one my limbs are forced down. Engorging, a red silhouette is the last thing I see.

152

Ravenous by Mark Young

The pain was excruciating. Madeline glanced at the hatch to the cellar. She'd get no help from the man upstairs. How on Earth was she supposed to take care of her offspring locked up in this devil's cesspit?

Her body collapsed as she pushed the last one out. She hadn't the strength to tear the umbilical cord with her teeth like she had with the others. But she didn't have to.

Something was chewing flesh.

All eight babies devoured the cord with their razor-sharp teeth. And when they were done, Madeline screamed as they ravenously crawled back towards the womb.

153

Witness by A.B. Archambault

"I swear to tell the truth…." Devereaux lowered his hand. That's how it always starts.

The middle was malleable. Today, truth was a numbers game, and the jurors were bad at math.

Then a child, mumbling some old rhyme… "cross my heart…" She had been there before.

Back at the hotel, Devereaux fiddled with the complimentary sewing kit. Words echoed in his mind, "stick a needle in my eye." He had lied.

The eye patch fell to the sink, revealing a scarred and milky orb. The needle slipped in fast and smooth.

"Hope to die." That's how it always ends.

154

Protect and Serve by Joshua Borgmann

Captain Anderson and his squad stormed into the duplex answering a report of Moneyless hiding in the structure. They were to save bullets. Axes would delivery enough lethal force at a cheaper rate.

As they burst in, he watched an officer cleave an old woman's face ending sixty years of waste. Quickly, the work appeared done, but as his men dragged a woman off, Anderson heard a cry from a closet. The girl he found reminded him of his five-year-old daughter. She cowered crying, but he showed no hesitation in driving his axe into her face.

No money; no mercy.

155

Rubble by Chris Bonner

Natalie slid down the South side of Sears Tower. Tumbled at the end, didn't even drop her Llama. Civilization's chalky remnants clog our nasal passages like a night of cocaine. The runes of rubble are ground so fine it cakes up inside of our mouths.

I stepped on a body wading through that cat litter. Bloated and yellow, the dust made the corpse resemble a chicken breast powdered with flour. The punch of spoiled meat brings everything you've eaten bubbling up your throat. I shudder thinking about how many more there must be. Beneath the coarse rubble they're the foundation now.

156

Eternal Beauty by Galina Trefil

"I've never seen such a persistent mustache," the electrologist gawked. "Not even on a man."

"Just get it over with," Angela scowled.

"You were here only last week and already everything's in full-on Chewbacca mode! You're like a Chia Pet!"

Vampires were eternally beautiful. Well, nobody had warned Angela before becoming one that, along with everything else in her body constantly regenerating, her facial hair would too.

Angela grabbed the woman by the throat. After finishing her lunch, as she licked the stray drops of blood from around her lips, she hoped that the next electrologist wouldn't be so rude.

About the Author

Thank you for reading our macabre drabbles collection and we hope you enjoyed! If you did, or even if not, if you could take a moment to write a short review it is always appreciated!

If you enjoyed this collection by the Macabre Ladies you can also check out our Holiday Horror Collection:

Dark X-Mas here
Dark Valentine here
Dark Solstice here

For upcoming releases you can follow us on Facebook here or our website here

As always, thanks for reading. Until next time!

xxx
  Eleanor Merry and Cassandra Angler
  The Macabre Ladies

You can connect with me on:

🌐 https://macabreladies.wixsite.com/website
📘 https://www.facebook.com/groups/macabreladies